When Your Parents Get a Divorce

WHEN YOUR PARENTS GET A DIVORCE

A Kid's Journal

BY ANN BANKS

Illustrated by Cathy Bobak

Puffin Books

Acknowledgments

*I would like to thank Elizabeth Austin and Cynthia Monahon
for their thoughtful suggestions on the manuscript.*

PUFFIN BOOKS
Published by the Penguin Group
Viking Penguin, a division of Penguin Books USA Inc.,
375 Hudson Street, New York, New York 10014, U.S.A.
Penguin Books Ltd, 27 Wrights Lane, London W8 5TZ, England
Penguin Books Australia Ltd, Ringwood, Victoria, Australia
Penguin Books Canada Ltd, 2801 John Street, Markham, Ontario, Canada L3R 1B4
Penguin Books (N.Z.) Ltd, 182–190 Wairau Road, Auckland 10, New Zealand

Penguin Books Ltd, Registered Offices: Harmondsworth, Middlesex, England

First published in Puffin Books 1990
1   3   5   7   9   10   8   6   4   2
Text copyright © Ann Banks, 1990
Illustrations copyright © Cathy Bobak, 1990
All rights reserved

Printed in the United States of America
Set in Times Roman

To Liz, Steve and the Mountain Brook Children's Center

When Your Parents Get a Divorce

About This Book

When parents can't live together happily anymore, sometimes they decide to get divorced. They stop being married and are no longer husband and wife. But they're still your father and mother, and they always will be. Parents may divorce each other, but they don't divorce their children.

If your parents are getting a divorce, the most important thing to remember is this: It's not your fault! Kids often feel that they're to blame for their parents' divorce. They might think if only they'd been better behaved, this never would have happened. It isn't true. Grown-ups get divorced for grown-up reasons— not because of their children. That also means that no matter how good you are, it won't bring your parents back together again.

There are probably a lot of questions in your mind. Who's going to take care of you? Where will you live? How will you celebrate holidays? Will you still get to see your grandparents? Will there be enough money? After your parents decide to live apart, everyone has to get used to big changes. That takes a long time, and so does the legal process of making the divorce official. Don't be surprised if your parents' divorce is the biggest thing on your mind for at least a year.

During that time, it's good to talk about what's happening—to your parents and your friends. You can also write down or draw what you feel. Filling in the pages of *When Your Parents Get a Divorce* can help you get through the hardest part. If you don't want to do everything in the book, don't. And if you feel like doing the projects in a different order, go ahead. Just think of the book as an extra friend, one you can confide in whenever you want.

Here is something to remember. Although a divorce is the end of many things, it's also a time of new beginnings. Sometimes it's a relief not to be living in an unhappy home with parents who aren't getting along. And you may find you have a closer relationship with one or both of your parents once they aren't together anymore.

Paste or draw a picture of yourself here.

This is Me.
And this is My Book.

All About Me

My name is_____

My friends call me_____

Other nicknames are_____

I am_____years old.

My address is_____

_____

I go to school at_____

I am in the_____grade.

My favorite teacher is_____

My Family

I have _____ brothers and _____ sisters.

Their names are _____

I am the _____ oldest _____ youngest _____ middle child.

My mother's name is _____

My father's name is _____

My grandparents on my father's side:

Names _____

Address _____

_____

Telephone number _____

My grandparents on my mother's side:

Names _____

Address _____

Telephone number _____

My Family

I have a pet named_____

This pet is a_____

A pet I would like to have is a_____

I would name this pet_____

Draw a picture of your family.

Finding Out About the Divorce

You might have known for quite a while that things weren't right in your house. Maybe you heard arguing; maybe your parents seemed sad or tense most of the time. Even if you've sometimes worried that your parents would get divorced, seeing these fears come true is a shock. You're likely to feel very lonesome and lost when you first hear the news. This may be hard to believe, but you won't always feel as bad as you do at first.

The way I found out about my parents' divorce was_____

_____

_____

The place I was when I found out was_____

The date was_____

The time of day was_____

My first thought was_____

The thing I'll always remember about that day is_____

_____

_____

14

Finding Out About the Divorce

The way I felt when I heard the news was _____

_____

_____

_____

Draw a picture of how you felt.

Why Are They Doing This?

People decide to end marriages for many different reasons. Some kids try to learn everything they can about why their parents are getting divorced. Other kids would rather not hear much about it. But even if you feel that way, ask your parents to give you a simple explanation. That way, you'll have something to say when people ask.

My mother says the reason for the divorce is_____

_____

_____

_____

I think the reason for the divorce is_____

_____

_____

_____

Why Are They Doing This?

My father says the reason for the divorce is_____

_____

_____

_____

How it Works

When people get a divorce, there are many arrangements that must be made—about money, about who will live where, and about how much time each parent will spend with you; about how possessions will be divided. You'll probably be interested in knowing who's going to end up with the TV, the stereo, the car. Often people get lawyers to help them settle these questions. Sometimes, when they can't reach an agreement, it's left up to a judge to decide. Since each divorce is different, ask one or both of your parents to explain to you how theirs is going to work.

What my father says about how their divorce will work is_____

_____

_____

_____

_____

_____

_____

_____

How it Works

What my mother says about how their divorce will work is_____

_____

_____

_____

_____

_____

_____

_____

_____

_____

_____

Telling People

Divorce happens to lots of kids, and it isn't anything to feel embarrassed or ashamed about. Still, it can be hard to tell people, especially in the beginning. It helps if you start by sharing your news with one close friend. Pick someone you can trust—maybe a kid whose parents are divorced, who can understand what you're going through. Once you start telling more people, you'll get used to saying the words and it will be a little easier. Don't be surprised if some people act strange at first. They may not know what to say, and so they end up saying something that hurts your feelings—like about how it's not so bad because at least you get twice as many presents on your birthday. Probably every kid whose parents are divorced has heard that one a couple of times.

Sometimes I'm afraid to tell people because_____

_____

The first friend I felt comfortable telling was_____

I felt comfortable telling him/her because_____

He / She said this about it_____

_____

A friend I told about the divorce was_____

He / She said this about it_____

_____

A friend I told about the divorce was_____

He / She said this about it_____

_____

Telling People

A friend I told about the divorce was_____

He / She said this about it_____

_____

The most helpful thing anyone said to me was_____

_____

_____

The least helpful thing anyone said was_____

_____

_____

Feelings

If you're like a lot of kids, your feelings about the divorce will change as time passes. After you get over the shock of hearing the news, you may even be relieved. If your parents have been arguing a lot, it might seem less tense in the house. Each person's experience is different, but most kids also go through a time of being angry at one or both of their parents—and even at the world. And then there are feelings of sadness that the family won't be together anymore, and that nothing will be the same.

Remember, you don't have to pretend things are okay when they're not. It's not your job to cheer everybody else up. If you're feeling shocked, angry, relieved, or sad—or if you're feeling some other way—write it down on the following pages.

It was a big shock when_____

_____

It was a big shock when_____

_____

It was a big shock when_____

_____

It was a big shock when_____

_____

I feel really sad when_____

_____

Feelings

I feel really sad when_____

_____

I feel really sad when_____

_____

I feel really sad when_____

_____

I feel really angry when_____

_____

I feel really angry when_____

_____

I feel really angry when_____

_____

I feel really angry when_____

_____

Feelings

I feel relieved because_____

_____

I feel relieved because_____

_____

I feel relieved because_____

_____

I feel relieved because_____

_____

I feel relieved because_____

_____

Feelings

I feel _____

_____

I feel _____

_____

I feel _____

_____

I feel _____

_____

Thoughts, Drawings, Dreams

As time goes by, and the way you feel about the divorce changes, turn back to these pages and write or draw what's on your mind. Put a date by each entry, so you can see how your feelings change. You'll probably find that it's not straight progress from sad to happy. Instead, there are many ups and downs. But gradually you'll sense a change for the better—your thoughts are more about *you* again and less about *them*.

Thoughts, Drawings, Dreams

How to Make Myself Feel Better

When your parents separate, the first weeks and months are the hardest. Your own feelings are as upset as can be, and your parents are going through their own hard times. But there are things you can do to help yourself feel better—and ways you can make yourself feel worse, too. Even if you want to, don't shut yourself off from people and mope around in your room for days at a time. It's hard, but push yourself to go out into the world. The ideas on this page have helped other kids whose parents were getting divorced.

Stay busy. Give yourself something to concentrate on besides the troubles at home.

> • Physical activity is a good idea—hard work or hard play. Get a job raking leaves or washing dishes. Do lots of sports. Join the swim team. Go out for track. Ride your bike. Kick a soccer ball around. Get as much exercise as you can.
>
> • Sometimes helping others is a good way to take your mind off your own problems. Sign up with a volunteer organization. Offer to run errands for a neighbor who has trouble getting around. Read to kids in the neighborhood.

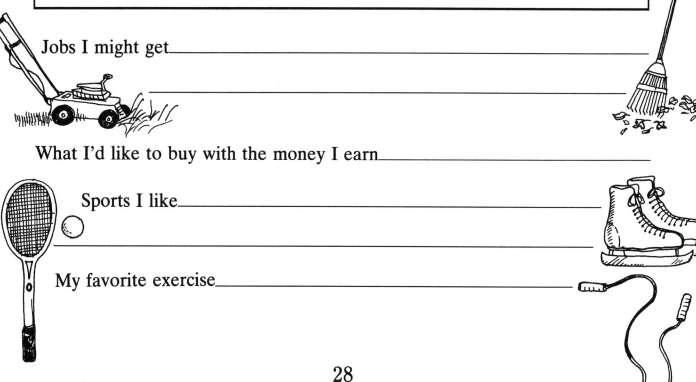

Jobs I might get_____

_____

What I'd like to buy with the money I earn_____

Sports I like_____

_____

My favorite exercise_____

How to Make Myself Feel Better

Volunteer activities I could do_____

_____

My hobbies are_____

_____

My after-school activities are_____

_____

My favorite way to let off steam is_____

_____

When I feel sad, I cheer myself up by_____

_____

A place I go that makes me feel good is_____

_____

The reason I like it is_____

_____

What Makes Me Happy

For a while, you may be too sad to enjoy doing some of your favorite things. But remember that happier moods will come again. When you're feeling good, what are the things you most look forward to?

Things I like to do are_____

_____

_____

_____

_____

_____

_____

_____

_____

What Makes Me Happy

Things I like to do are_____

_____

_____

_____

_____

_____

_____

_____

_____

Who Can I Talk To?

Find someone to talk to. If you have friends whose parents are divorced, they'll know what you're going through. (Just remember that your experience won't be exactly the same as anyone else's.) Aunts and uncles, grandparents or other relatives can be helpful, especially because they know you and your parents. Also, you might want to talk to a grown-up outside your family—your favorite teachers, a school counselor, a scout leader. If they can't help you, they probably will be able to suggest someone who can.

The people who have helped me the most:

Name _____ Phone number_____

What he / she says is_____

_____

_____

_____

Name _____ Phone number_____

What he / she says is_____

_____

_____

_____

Who Can I Talk To?

Name _____ Phone number_____

What he / she says is_____

_____

_____

_____

Name _____ Phone number_____

What he / she says is_____

_____

_____

_____

Name _____ Phone number_____

What he / she says is_____

_____

_____

_____

Worries

Whatever is bothering you, sometimes it's easier to write it down than to talk about it. If you want your parents to know what's on your mind, you can show them these pages.

Here are things other kids have worried about when their parents divorced:
*What if my mom has to go on a business trip? Who will take care of me?
*What if we have to move and leave the dog behind?
*What if my birthday comes and I don't get to see both my parents?
*What if my dad feels too sad and lonely when I go stay with my mom?
*What if we don't have enough money to take a vacation?

Fill in some what-ifs of your own.

What if _____

_____

_____

_____

What if _____

_____

_____

_____

What if _____

_____

_____

Worries

What if

Sisters and Brothers

If you're like a lot of kids whose parents are going through a divorce, you might end up getting closer to your sisters and brothers. Try talking to them about what's going on in the family.

My sister says_____

_____

_____

My sister says_____

_____

_____

My brother says_____

_____

_____

My brother says_____

_____

Parents Are People

The decision to separate is very hard for parents, as well as for kids. Just when you need your parents most, it may seem that they are putting more time and energy into their own problems. And in the beginning especially, you may hear crying and arguing. But try to remember that things probably will get better eventually, and the sad mood won't last forever.

This is a good time to begin thinking of each of your parents as a separate person. You may find that you're like your mother in certain ways, and in other ways, you're like your father. But of course the one you're most like is yourself.

My Mother is . . .

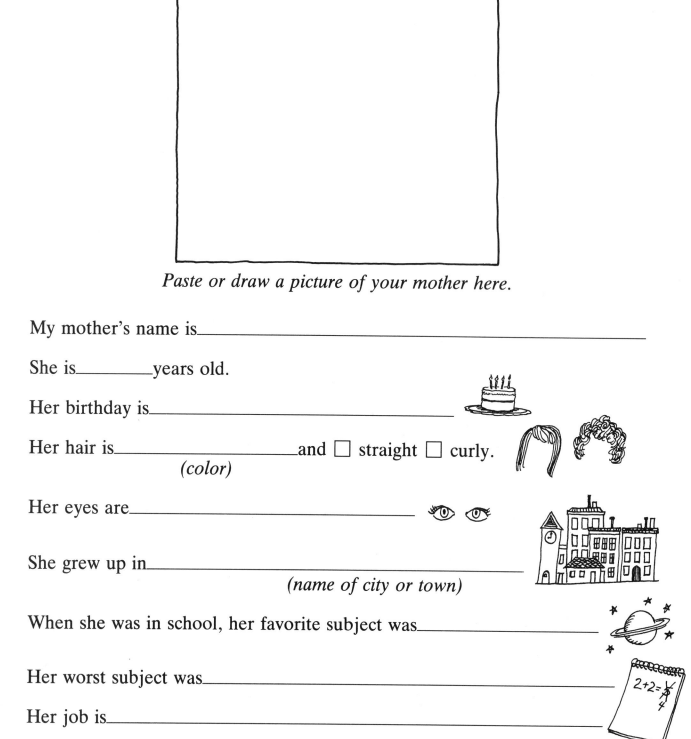

Paste or draw a picture of your mother here.

My mother's name is_____

She is_____years old.

Her birthday is_____

Her hair is_____and ☐ straight ☐ curly.
              (color)

Her eyes are_____

She grew up in_____
                    (name of city or town)

When she was in school, her favorite subject was_____

Her worst subject was_____

Her job is_____

My Mother is . . .

Her secret ambition is _____

_____

Sports she likes are _____

On vacation, her favorite thing to do is _____

_____

The way she likes to spend Saturdays is _____

The kind of music she likes is _____

The kind of books she enjoys reading are _____

When she was a kid, her favorite book was _____

Her favorite movies are _____

Her favorite TV show is _____

The kind of food she likes best is _____

Given a choice, she'd rather live in: ☐ city ☐ country ☐ suburbs.

Her biggest hope for me is that _____

_____

_____

My Father is . . .

Paste or draw a picture of your father here.

My father's name is_____

He is_____years old.

His birthday is_____

His hair is_____and ☐ straight ☐ curly.
　　　　　　　　(color)

His eyes are_____

He grew up in_____
　　　　　　　(name of city or town)

When he was in school, his favorite subject was_____

His worst subject was_____

His job is_____

My Father is . . .

His secret ambition is

Sports he likes are

On vacation, his favorite thing to do is

The way he likes to spend Saturdays is

The kind of music he likes is

The kind of books he enjoys reading are

When he was a kid, his favorite book was

His favorite movies are

His favorite TV show is

The kind of food he likes best is

Given a choice, he'd rather live in: ☐ city ☐ country ☐ suburbs.

His biggest hope for me is that

I am . . .

My name is_____

I am_____years old.

My birthday is_____

My hair is_____and ☐ straight ☐ curly.
              (color)

My eyes are_____

I'm growing up in_____
                    (name of city of town)

My favorite subject in school is_____

My worst subject is_____

My secret ambition is_____

_____

Sports I like are_____

Things I'm especially good at are_____

_____

On vacation, my favorite thing to do is_____

_____

I am . . .

The way I like to spend Saturdays is _____

The kind of music I like is _____

The kind of books I enjoy reading are _____

My favorite book is _____

My favorite movies are _____

My favorite TV show is _____

The kind of food I like best is _____

Given a choice, I'd rather live in: ☐ city ☐ country ☐ suburbs.

My biggest hope for myself is that _____

_____

_____

What Will Happen to Me?

You probably have lots of questions about what life will be like when your parents aren't together anymore. It's not always easy to get clear answers. Sometimes parents are so upset that they have a hard time explaining what will happen. If you're not sure you understand what you're hearing from them, say so. Say, "I don't know what you mean. Could you explain that to me another way?"

Also, your parents may not know everything yet. Until they come to an agreement about how the divorce is going to work, life can be very confusing. Probably a lot of things still aren't definite. But keep asking questions. Make a list, and as you think of new questions, write them down. Even if your parents don't have all the answers yet, at least they'll know what's on your mind.

After my parents separate, I will:

_____ go to a new school.   _____ go to the same school.

What will happen to my pet is_____

My schedule:

The days I will be with my mom are_____

_____

The days my brothers and sisters will be with my mom are_____

My mom's address is_____

_____

Her phone number at home is_____

Her phone number at work is_____

I can call her there_____ any time I want_____ only with permission.

The way I get to my mom's is_____

What Will Happen to Me?

The room I'll stay in when I'm there is_____

The way I will decorate the room is_____

The things I'll have to play with there are_____

_____

The days I will be with my dad are_____

_____

The days my brothers and sisters with be with my dad are_____

My dad's address is_____

_____

His phone number at home is_____

His phone number at work is_____

I can call him there_____ any time I want_____ only with permission.

The way I get to my dad's is_____

The room I'll stay in when I'm there is_____

The way I will decorate the room is_____

The things I'll play with there are_____

_____

The distance between my father's home and my mother's home is_____

_____ miles.

More Questions

My Mother's Home, My Father's Home

Going back and forth between two houses takes some getting used to. There are many different ways it can work. Sometimes kids live with one parent during the week and the other on weekends. Sometimes the time is split up between the school year and vacations. Partly, this will depend on whether your parents will still be living in the same city. At first you might feel shy or strange when you spend time with one or the other of your parents. The best way to get over this is for you to be around each other—and to do normal, everyday things together.

Once your parents are living apart, their differences probably will become more obvious. They'll each have their own interests and moods. And they'll probably have different ideas about you—how much you should help around the house, how neat you should keep things. Also, parents may change after the separation, sometimes in ways that you like. Think about starting new traditions—special things that you do together when you're with each parent. Perhaps you could start a tropical fish aquarium, or make a regular pancake breakfast on the weekend, or plant a garden.

My father likes an atmosphere that is_____

_____

He thinks neatness is_____

_____

Chores I do at my father's home are_____

_____

The place I sleep at my father's home is_____

Things my father and I like to do together are_____

_____

47

My Mother's Home, My Father's Home

My favorite thing I've done with my father is_____

_____

Something my father and I want to do together is_____

_____

Places I've visited with my father are_____

_____

Places we'd like to go together are_____

_____

My mother likes an atmosphere that is_____

_____

She thinks neatness is_____

_____

Chores I do at my mother's home are_____

_____

My Mother's Home, My Father's Home

The place I sleep at my mother's home is _____

Things my mother and I like to do together are _____

_____

My favorite thing I've done with my mother is _____

_____

Something my mother and I want to do together is _____

_____

Places I've visited with my mother are _____

_____

Places we'd like to go together are _____

_____

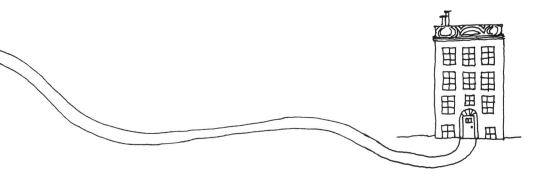

Speaking Up

Even if they don't mean to, sometimes your parents might do things that make you feel uncomfortable. For example:

—If your dad criticizes your mom or the other way around.
—Or if one parent gives you a message to take to the other.
—Or asks you a lot of questions when you come back from a visit.
—Or doesn't give you privacy when you're talking on the phone to the other parent.
—Or if both parents talk about private things where you can hear them.

Learning to stand up for yourself is never easy. But it's important to be brave enough to talk to your parents in a respectful way when there's something you'd like to change. Try writing down how you feel. Then maybe it will be easier to say it.

It makes me feel uncomfortable when_____

_____

It makes me feel uncomfortable when_____

_____

It makes me feel uncomfortable when_____

_____

It makes me feel uncomfortable when_____

_____

Feeling Proud

When your parents decided to get a divorce, nobody asked for your opinion. They made up their minds what to do, and you had to figure out how to live through it. It's hard to believe in the beginning, but having your parents divorce can lead to you becoming a stronger person. Sometimes kids say they're not as bothered by small stuff anymore. Or that they're more sensitive to other kids who are having problems. What are some of the things you're proud of yourself for?

I'm proud of myself because_____

_____

_____

I'm proud of myself because_____

_____

_____

Remembering

You probably have happy memories from when the family was together—before the divorce. It's okay to remember these special times, even if it makes you feel sad. Everything may have changed, but you don't have to give up the good memories. If you want, write some of them down here.

I remember when _____

_____

_____

_____

_____

I remember when _____

_____

_____

_____

_____

Remembering

I remember when _____

_____

_____

_____

_____

My Advice is . . .

Pretend you met a kid who just found out his parents were getting a divorce. What would you tell him about divorce? What are the worst things about it? And the best things? What's the most important thing to remember?

My Advice is . . .

A Parents' Guide

to *When Your Parents Get A Divorce*

A Parents' Guide

Under any circumstances, divorce is difficult, untidy, painful. In families with children, the sadness is multiplied. Children have no say in the decision when a marriage ends. They may hate the idea, yet they must learn to live with the changes it brings. How will the divorce affect them? What will help them weather the storm? It isn't easy for recently separated parents to find answers to these questions—especially at a time when they're dealing with their own emotional turmoil. Yet with a divorce in the works, children need support and guidance more than ever. (Since fifty percent of all marriages now end in divorce, your child probably won't be the only one in the class who doesn't live with both parents.)

When Your Parents Get a Divorce is a combination journal and activity book. It's filled with projects for kids to do, starting from the time they first learn about the separation until they've begun assimilating the experience, and can give advice to others in a similar situation. The book invites children to express and order their feelings as they chronicle the difficult early weeks and months of separation. It encourages them to ask questions about what will happen, to put into words their secret fears, to learn to see each parent separately, to find people to confide in, and to develop their own strategies for coping: physical activity, helping others, writing about their feelings in *When Your Parents Get a Divorce*.

Some of the pages children will complete on their own; others are designed to be filled in with the help of an adult. By using *When Your Parents Get a Divorce* as a starting point, family members can more easily discuss the emotionally-charged issues that inevitably arise. Also, since the child participates in creating *When Your Parents Get a Divorce*, the book becomes an important personal possession—one that can offer comfort in a sad and stressful time.

Each child will react differently to a divorce, depending on various factors such as age, birth order, family circumstances, and temperament. But there is a great deal parents can do to ease the adjustment. The suggestions that follow have been distilled from published research on children and divorce, from interviews with experts on child development, and from conversations with parents and children themselves.

*Take pains to reassure your kids that they are not to blame for the divorce. Children, especially younger children, often are convinced that it's all their fault, and that if they'd been better behaved, this never would have happened. They may also believe that if only they can behave perfectly *now,* perhaps they can bring their parents back together again. Do your best to correct these misconceptions.

*Explain the divorce to your children at least every six months. One explanation is not enough. As time goes by, their ability to understand what you tell them will change, and they'll have new questions and concerns.

*Don't give up on setting limits. When your children are going through a difficult time, it's tempting to relax standards of behavior—especially if you're feeling guilty about disrupting their lives. But discipline is part of love, and it's important for kids of divorcing parents to know that they're being looked after as closely as before. At such an unsettled time, consistency is especially important.

*Discourage your children from taking sides. And try to refrain from making bitter remarks about your ex-spouse where they can hear you. Children usually take after both parents. So they're apt to interpret a criticism of one of their parents—no matter how justified—as a criticism of them, as well.

*Resist the temptation to confide in your children. In the short run, it may make them feel flattered and grown-up. But they don't really want to hear about your troubles, and in the long run, they're likely to resent it. You *will* need to talk about what's happening, so make an effort to find adult confidants.

*Don't make your children feel guilty about enjoying themselves with their other parent. You may be annoyed at your ex-spouse for lavishing treats on the kids. You may feel hurt that you aren't in a position to do the same. But try to set these feelings aside temporarily when dealing with your children. Eventually they'll sort things out and draw their own conclusions.

*Respect the privacy of your children's relationship with your ex-spouse. Do your best not to pry when children return from a visit. Allow them privacy for phone conversations with their other parent. Don't use the kids to carry messages, letters, or checks between yourself and your ex-spouse.

*Try to help your kids maintain a relationship with relatives on both sides. When parents are in the middle of a divorce, the extended family of grandparents, aunts, uncles, and cousins often becomes more important to children than ever.

*Establish new traditions for holiday celebrations. More than any other times, holidays and birthdays remind kids that things will never be the same. Instead of ending up with a pale imitation of occasions past, try to do something entirely different. And be sure to make it something that you'll enjoy, as well. The happier you are, the more likely it is that your kids will be happy.

*Encourage your children to stick up for themselves. It's especially important that children whose parents are divorced learn to talk about what's bothering them. Let your kids know that if there's something on their mind, you'd like to hear about it. But don't be too pushy about this—kids need to have their privacy respected.

Once completed, *When Your Parents Get a Divorce* will have eased your child's adjustment to a stressful experience. In the months and years to come, it can serve as a comforting reminder of survival in the face of adversity.

In his autobiography, the writer Reynolds Price said these were the words he most wanted to hear as a child: "This bad afternoon, and your feelings about it, is painful but it's already ending—look, the sun is going down; soon you'll be asleep. Time keeps moving. Nothing stays the same and you'll be better soon." Perhaps the most reassuring message you can give your children is that time heals, and that they won't always feel as bad as they do now.